The Grand Adventures of

Paddy and Fenway

By Patricia Gonzalez
contributions by
Patrick N Armstrong
illustrated by Ciro W Romero

ISBN: 1500955078
ISBN 13: 9781500955076

For the Good Lord

Our Nieces and Nephews: *Celeste, Sophia, Mia, Michael, Loren, Elena, Evan, Nora, Joseph, James, Abigail, Mary-Kathryn, Jack, Caroline, Ava, Eric Jon, Micaela, Cataleya and Zoe*

Our Parents: Mercedes, Joaquin, Kathryn and Norman

Our Siblings: Priscila, Michael, Lorenzo, Robyn, William and Karalyn

If you can dream it, you can achieve it.

An Irish Blessing:

May God grant you always,

A sunbeam to warm you,

A moonbeam to charm you,

A sheltering Angel so nothing can harm you,

Laughter to cheer you,

And whenever you pray, Heaven to hear you.

Table of Contents

A BOY ON A MISSION

Once upon a time, in a land far, far away in Cranston, Rhode Island, there lived an 8-year-old boy named Patrick. He was a very curious boy, always looking around his house for clues that would lead to great treasures and adventures. He would search in his room, in the basement, under the cupboard, in the laundry basket, in his sisters' room, in his mother's flower garden, and even in his brother's stinky gym bag.

"Patrick! Get out of there!" his mother would yell.

But Patrick wouldn't listen. He kept on searching, looking high and low for his next adventure. Then on one fateful summer day, Patrick noticed a shiny object on top of the fireplace.

"A clue! A clue!" he yelled. "It's the missing piece of the puzzle map that will lead me to the buried treasure." Patrick tried to reach it, but he was just too small.

He ran to his brother to ask for help. "Billy, Billy, I need your help getting my treasure," he yelled.

"Get out of here, squirt. Can't you see I'm busy playing my video games?" his brother screamed.

But that didn't stop Patrick. "I know. I'll try Kaitlin and Rosie. They have to help me." Off he ran to find his twin sisters, but they were nowhere in sight. Patrick sighed as he stood in front of the fireplace, staring at the shiny object. "How am I ever going to get that clue?" he said. Then he had an idea. "I know! I'll just build a ladder out of the building blocks in my room." So off he went, dragging all of his blocks across the house and to the living room.

"What are you doing, Paddy?" his mother asked with a concerned look on her face.

"Oh nothing, Mom. I'm just playing," Patrick said, giving his mom a huge smile, hoping she wouldn't suspect a thing.

"Just playing, huh? OK, Patrick. Just be careful. I would hate to have to visit Dr. Gonzalez again."

One block, two blocks, three blocks, four—Patrick was high atop of his wobbly blocks. "Allllmooost...got...it...Whoa!" *Crash! Bang! Boom!* Patrick and his blocks came tumbling down.

"Oooouch, my arm," Patrick cried.

"What happened? What did you do this time?" his mother cried, running into the room.

In an instant, his family surrounded Patrick. "Oooouch, my arm!" Patrick cried out again, this time with tears in his eyes.

"Not again," said Patrick's father. "OK, everybody, you know the drill. Outside and into the car. Let's go. Let's go!" Out the door and into the station wagon they went—Mom, Dad, Billy, Kaitlin, Rosie, and poor, poor Patrick, holding his aching arm.

Off to the doctor they sped. At the office, Nurse Michelle greeted Patrick. "Paddy boy, what happened now? Another one of your wild adventures?" she asked, smiling.

"Yes, but this time my arm really hurts," groaned Patrick with tears in his eyes.

"Come with me," Nurse Michelle said as she led Patrick to an examination room to take his X-rays and get him ready for the doctor.

This day wasn't looking well for poor Paddy boy. When Dr. Gonzalez arrived to the examination room with his X-rays in her hand, she already knew she was in for a treat when it came to Patrick. He always described what had happened to him as if he were still treasure hunting.

"Paddy boy! Good to see you, but I see here that you broke your arm. What happened? Was it the ghosts again? Or was it the space aliens?" Dr. Gonzalez asked Patrick anxiously.

"Well," Patrick began, as his parents and the doctor watched and listened, "I was in the Amazon, searching for the next clue in my puzzle map. I looked for it in the first cave, but there was a monster playing video games there; then I tried looking in the cave of the two-headed beast, but it wasn't there either. Then I found it in the cave of fire! It was high up on a ledge, but I couldn't reach it. So I took a bunch of rocks and made a ladder, but I fell off and hurt my arm."

"I see," said the doctor as she smiled and patted him on the head. "Well, Paddy boy, your arm will have to be in a cast for the rest of the summer. That means *no swimming, no biking, no running, no jumping, no playgrounds,* and most important of all, *no treasure hunting.*"

A BOY AND HIS DOG

Patrick sighed and frowned. His entire summer was ruined. "Aww man," he said as he stared down at his cast.

"Did you hear that, Patrick? *No treasure hunting!*" his mother said with a stern look on her face.

When they arrived home, his parents took him to his room and tucked him into bed. "OK, son, time to rest. No treasure hunting until further notice." His dad said sternly.

This all made Patrick very sad. But he knew he'd return to his treasure hunt the minute he could. The rest of the week was gloomy and rainy. With a broken arm and rainy weather, all Patrick could do was sit in his room and stare out the window. He tried coloring and drawing, but it wasn't any fun. He tried playing with his toy cars, but it just wasn't the same. "I wish I had someone to play with," he said sadly. "Just someone who can come with me on my adventures and help me find all that buried treasure."

All he could do was sit and think of his next adventure. Then one afternoon, there was a knock on his bedroom door.

"Come in," he yelled, but no one opened the door. "I said come in!" Still, he heard nothing, not even a sound. He got up and went to his door, but there was no one. As he started to close his door, he noticed a piece of paper taped on the outside. He tore it off and looked: it was a treasure map!

"A map! A map! And it has instructions," Patrick shouted. Then he read aloud, "Follow the arrows and you will see...a path laid out for thee. Under the mountains of pillows you will find...a surprise to help you pass your time."

"*Trrreeeaaasssuuurre!*" shouted Patrick with excitement. He hadn't felt this happy since his last hunt. Off he went with his map in hand to find the treasure that awaited him. As he walked, he wondered what it could be; his mind raced with each turn he took. Then he found himself in front of his treasure.

His family sneaked into the living room and watched him fling the mountain of pillows all around him. He came upon a box with a huge bow and a card that said, "To Paddy boy: Here's a friend to play with until you can go on your adventures again. We were told that he is a very special boy. Take good care of him, and he'll take good care of you. Love always, Mom and Dad." As he opened the box, out popped a white puppy with a brown face and a little white tail.

"Ah! A puppy," screamed Patrick, so loudly that the neighbors heard him outside. "I got a puppy!" Patrick's family gazed at him with big smiles.

"Now you have someone to protect you on your hunts," said Dad.

"But you're in charge of feeding him and taking him outside," said Mom.

"I promise to love and protect him and pick up his poop. I'll be on poop duty. He'll be my adventure buddy!" said Patrick proudly.

"What're you going to name him?" asked Dad.

Patrick thought long and hard. He thought of all of the doggie names he'd heard of—Rocco, Bogan, Potter and Herbert—but none of these worked. This dog was special. So it had to have a special name. He thought of all the things that were special to him. "Hmmm...umm..." he wondered aloud.

As he looked around the living room for ideas, he spotted a picture of himself and his dad at their first-ever baseball game. It was Patrick's favorite day. He'd gone to Fenway Park in Boston, Massachusetts, with his dad for the first time to see the Boston Red Sox play. He remembered the hour-long car ride like it was yesterday; it was the longest car ride ever! Patrick had been so excited to see all of his favorite baseball players. That day, he'd gotten to eat ice cream, hot dogs, and roasted peanuts, and he even caught a foul ball. It was a new tradition that he'd begun with his father.

"Oh, I know. Fenway! I'll name him Fenway," said Patrick while petting his new puppy.

"Fenway? Hmm, I like it!" said Mom.

"Fenway! We can call him Fen for short," said Dad.

Patrick was over the moon with his new dog. He grabbed Fenway, quickly hurried off to his room, and got to work drawing a picture of the two of them. He couldn't wait to show all of his friends that he'd gotten a puppy during summer vacation. As he sat at his desk, a small voice rang out. "What are you doing?" the voice asked.

Patrick looked around to see who was there, but it was only Fenway and him.

"What are you doing?" the voice asked again.

Patrick looked around and then down at Fenway and said, "Boy, Fenway, I think I'm hearing voices."

"What are you doing up there?" Fenway asked. Patrick stared at Fenway, shaking his head. He couldn't believe what he was seeing. His new friend could talk. "Are you playing a game?" Fenway continued, eagerly wagging his tail. "I love games. Are you drawing a picture? I love pictures."

Patrick couldn't believe his eyes and ears. "You...you...you can talk?" he asked.

"Only you can understand me. No one else can," Fenway replied.

"Not even my mom? Dad? Or my stinky brother?" he asked.

"Nope! Only you," Fenway replied.

"Wicked!" shouted Patrick.

"Patrick, are you OK in there?" his mother called in to him.

"Yes, Mom, I'm fine," he replied. "Fenway, how is it you can talk?" Patrick asked in a low voice so his mother wouldn't hear.

"Well," said Fenway, "I come from a place of pure love; a place where wishes and dreams are made. Deep down inside, you really wanted a friend, someone to go with you on your adventures. So I was sent here. To you." Patrick grabbed Fenway and hugged him tightly. Fenway licked his face.

"So where are we off to next, Paddy?" Fenway asked, his tail wagging excitedly.

"Well, I was on the hunt for buried treasure in the jungles of the Amazon," said Patrick excitedly.

"The Amazon? Where is that?" Fenway asked with his head turned to the side.

"I'll show you." With that, Patrick crawled up onto his bed and pointed to a spot on the map that hung over him. "It's right there, in South America.

It's a big place full of huge trees and all sorts of animals. But right in the middle of it," he said as he pointed, "that's where the treasure is. A big chest full of diamonds, gold, and doggie treats. I'm afraid we can't go, though," he said sadly. "The doctor said no treasure hunts."

Fenway looked at Patrick and lay on the ground, slowly wagging his tail as he thought long and hard about the treasure hunt. He knew there had to be a way to find those buried treats. "Hmm, what if we closed our eyes and pretended to fly over there? Or pretended to be on a ship and sailed?" Patrick suggested.

"I've got it," Fenway said. "We can tail it."

"Tail it?" Patrick asked as he scratched his head.

"Yeah," Fenway said. "You see, as long as we know where we're going, my tail can take us there. All you have to do is hold on tight, say the magic words as I wiggle my tail fast, and we can go anywhere we want."

Patrick's eyes grew bigger and bigger as Fenway spoke. He wanted to yell with excitement, but he didn't want his parents to hear. "Let's do it. We can call it the Fenway Wiggle," Patrick whispered to Fenway.

"OK," said Fenway as he ran over to Patrick excitedly and got into position to go.

"So what *exactly* do we have to do? What are the magic words?" Patrick asked nervously.

"Well, you have to hold on to me tightly and just imagine exactly where you want to go. Then, on the count of three, you say, 'Let's go to the place where adventures grow,'" said Fenway.

"Sweet," said Patrick. "But before we go, I have to get some stuff." Patrick scurried around his room, putting on his adventure hat and adventure belt, filled with a rope, compass, flashlight, and his favorite snack, jelly beans. "OK, I'm ready, Fen," he said excitedly. Patrick knew that in a few moments, he was going to a place where all his wildest dreams would come true. He knew he was finally going to become a famous adventurer.

With gear in hand, Patrick knelt down next to Fenway and wrapped his arms around him. "OK, Fenway, *let's go!*" he exclaimed.

Fenway began to wag his tail slowly at first, wiggling it from left to right. "OK, Paddy. Grab onto me and get ready to say the magic words. On the count of three: one...two...three," he said.

Together, Patrick and Fenway closed their eyes and said the magic words, "Let's go to the place where adventures *grooooooow!*"

THE PLACE WHERE ADVENTURES GROW

Patrick and Fenway were suddenly thrown forward into a tunnel of bright lights and colors. Patrick had never seen so many colors in his entire life. His crayon box didn't even have that many colors. Suddenly, everything became very green, and there was a loud *thump!* Patrick and Fenway hit the ground rolling.

"Whoa!" they yelled simultaneously as they rolled onto the jungle floor. Patrick opened his eyes. Bushes, trees, and leaves surrounded him. He looked down to see his knees covered with dirt. Fenway was nowhere in sight.

"Fenway?" Patrick called out as he lay on the ground. "Are you OK?"

"Yeah," Fenway replied from within one of the bushes. He was lying on his side, attempting to catch his breath.

"That...was...wicked cool!" Patrick yelled as he shot up to his feet.

"I know!" yelled Fenway.

As Patrick stood up, he was amazed to see all the beauty that surrounded him in the middle of the Amazon jungle. He saw trees taller than the tallest buildings he'd ever seen in all of Rhode Island. He saw birds of all kinds flying around him as lizards looked at him and Fenway from the tree branches nearby. He saw the greenest greens, bluest blues, and reddest reds in the flowers that surrounded them. "Fenway, this is awesome," Patrick exclaimed.

"This place is really cool, Paddy boy," said Fenway as he made his way toward Patrick.

"Well, what should we do next?" Patrick asked.

"The map. We need to look at the map. Quick, Paddy, let me see your cast," said Fenway. Patrick held his arm out to Fenway with a puzzled look on his face. "Hold it steady," Fenway urged as he began to lick Patrick's cast.

"Ew! Fen, that's so gr—" but before he could finish his sentence, a map began to appear on his cast. "Whoa, how'd you do that, Fen?" asked Patrick as his eyes lit up.

"It's just a little magic, kiddo," Fenway said as he proudly wagged his tail. They eagerly gathered around the map as it revealed itself. "Let's see," said Fenway. "We are in the Valley of *Mucho Colores* now."

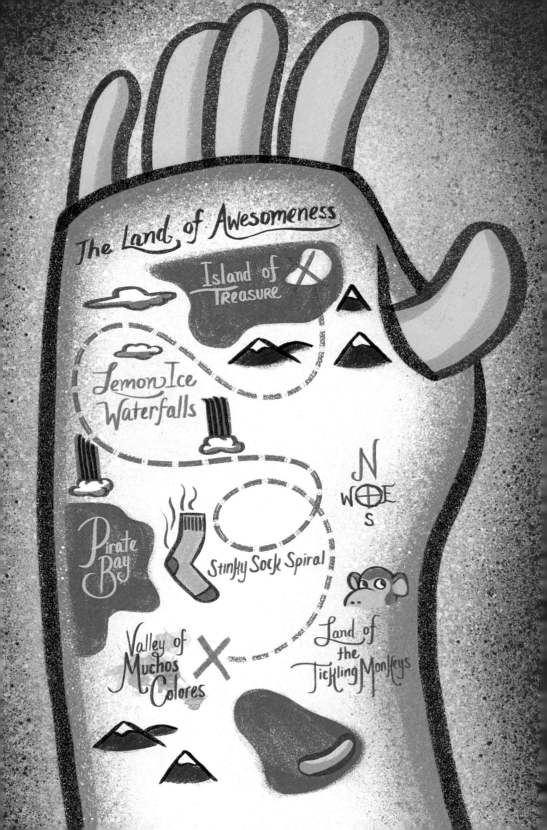

"What does *moo-cho co-lo-res* mean?" Patrick asked with a puzzled look on his face.

"It's Spanish. It means a 'lot of colors,'" Fenway replied. "So, all we have to do is follow the map. We go out of the Valley of Mucho Colores, through the Land Of The Tickling Monkeys, past the Stinky Sock Spiral, past the Lemon Ice Waterfalls, and we'll get right to the treasure," Fenway exclaimed.

"But what about Pirate Bay?" Patrick asked as he pointed to it on the map.

"Well, we'll have to be very careful there. Who knows what we might encounter. But no need to worry. We're in this together," Fenway reassured Patrick.

"OK, Fen, let's get started on this treasure hunt," he said as he got ready to start off.

"Let's go," said Fenway, happily wagging his tail.

THE LAND OF THE MONKEYS

Together they set off in the direction of their treasure. But little did they know that this would be no ordinary treasure hunt. They were about to encounter some of the wildest things that lurked in that part of the jungle. This would be one adventure they'd never forget.

As Patrick and Fenway walked deeper into the jungle, the sound of the monkeys grew louder and louder. *"Oooh oooh oooh! Aaah aaah aaah!"* Louder and louder the noises grew until the duo arrived at the Land of the Tickling Monkeys—a land covered in mist and full of laughing monkeys.

"Fe-Fenway?" said Patrick nervously. "Are you...are you scared?" he asked.

"Nope. As long as we stick together, there's nothing to be afraid of," Fen replied as he made his way to Patrick and licked the boy's face.

"OK, Fen, it's now or never," said Patrick bravely.

With that, Fenway and Patrick began walking into the misty land. The noises grew louder and louder the deeper

in they walked. Shadows began to move all around them. The monkeys swung from tree to tree, plotting their tickle attack. Patrick and Fenway moved as quickly as they could while watching each other's backs. Then suddenly there was a loud *thump* in front of them. They stopped. The mist cleared. Before them was the biggest gorilla they'd ever seen! Patrick and Fenway looked at each other nervously, and then back at the gorilla.

"Where do you think yoooou're going?" bellowed the gorilla. "How dare you come into my land unannounced."

"Sorry, sir," said Fenway. "We're just trying to get to the Stinky Sock Spiral."

"Who gave you permission to come through my land? This is the land of King Haha, the ruler of the tickling monkeys. Anyone who trespasses must pay the price," yelled the king.

"But...but...but we didn't mean to trespass, sir, uh, King... King Haha," Patrick exclaimed.

"Silence! You have trespassed, and now you must pay the price. Moooonkeeeys...start tickling!" he commanded.

Patrick and Fenway backed up into each other. They looked all around them. The trees began to sway and the ground began to shake as the army of monkeys made their way toward them.

"Quick, Fen! What do we do?" Patrick asked frantically.

"I don't know! I'm thinking. I'm thinking. We need something to distract them," Fenway suggested.

Suddenly, there were two loud *thumps*. Patrick and Fenway were knocked to the ground. The tickling had commenced. It seemed like all hope was lost.

"H a h a h a h a h h h a h a h a h a h a h a h a h a   o h hahahahahahahahahaha," bellowed Patrick as the monkeys tickled away.

"Oohhh ahahahahahahahahahaaaaaa!" chuckled Fenway as he struggled to pry himself loose from the monkeys.

"Yes, little monkeys. Don't...stop...tiiiiiiickliiiiiing!" King Haha bellowed.

The monkeys tickled them everywhere: on their heads, behind the ears, on their bellies, on their sides, and even in their armpits! Tickle, tickle, tickle, tickle!

"Fen—hahahahaha—we—hahahahaha—we—hahahahah—must—ohhhh hahahaha—do something!" Patrick said as he tried to catch his breath.

"I—hahahaha—know—hahahaha—we—hahahaha—need—hahahahaha—a—hahahaha—distraction!" said

Fenway with tears running down his cheeks as the monkeys tickled his belly.

Suddenly, Patrick remembered the jelly beans in his adventure belt. He tried frantically to reach them, laughing as hard as he ever had. Then, with a swift move, he grabbed a handful of jelly beans out of his belt and held them out to the monkeys. The monkeys stopped tickling. The land fell silent. He couldn't believe it had worked. He moved his hand from side to side, and the monkeys followed the movement.

"Fen! Fen! Look. They like the jelly beans," he whispered to Fenway.

"Great! Stay as still as possible, Paddy boy. On my count you're going to throw them behind you, and we're going to run out of here," Fenway whispered back.

"What's going on here, monkeys? Why have you—" the king began to yell, until he caught sight of the bright jelly beans. "What...is...that?" he asked.

"On the count of three, Paddy. One...two...three," yelled Fenway.

Patrick threw the jelly beans as hard and as fast as he could. The monkeys—and even the king—yelled and gave chase to the bright jelly beans. Patrick and Fenway ran as fast as they could in the opposite direction. The sound of the monkeys began to fade the farther they got.

WHAT'S THAT SMELL?

Fenway and Patrick ran far and fast. They could no longer hear monkeys when they finally decided to stop running.

"That was *crazy!*" said Patrick, panting.

"It was insane. I couldn't stop laughing," said Fenway as he lay on the ground, trying to catch his breath. "Great job with the jelly beans, Paddy boy. Where did you even get them?"

"I never leave home without them. They're my favorite snack when I'm on my hunts," he said as he made his way over to Fenway.

"I love snacks. I can't wait to get to the treasure. I'm sure there are all sorts of treats in there for us," Fenway said as he closed his eyes and imagined all the yummy doggie treats waiting for him.

"Yeah, me too," said Patrick as he stared off into the sky, dreaming about all the jewels, gold coins, and jelly beans waiting for him. "OK, so where are we headed to next? I hope not to another valley full of monkeys. I don't think I can handle being tickled again," said Patrick with a shudder.

"Well, let's check out the map. Stick out your arm and let's take a look," said Fenway.

Together they looked at Patrick's cast and followed the trail they'd started on. Their next destination wasn't a fun one. It was definitely different from the monkeys. This place seemed almost unbearable to think of.

"Oooh noooo," said Fenway slowly as his perky ears flopped down and his tail stopped wagging. "Stinky socks don't sound like they're fun," he said as he peered up at Patrick.

"Stinky socks are *not* fun," said Patrick. "One time my brother left his stinky socks in his gym bag for a week. He stunk up his room so bad that every time he opened the bedroom door, the whole house stunk," he said, shaking his head at the memory.

"Geez," Fenway said. "I sure hope we can make it out of there without fainting."

"All we need is a plan," Patrick said with a thoughtful look on his face.

The boys walked together in silence, slowly making their way toward the stinky socks. They were both in deep thought. What would they do once they arrived? How would they make it through the spiral? The smell of the socks was becoming stronger.

"What are we going to do, Paddy boy?" Fenway asked with a concerned look on his face.

"I don't know, Fen," Patrick said as he stared out in front of him. He could see and smell the entrance to the Stinky Sock Spiral.

They stopped walking and leaned against a giant tree with leaves as big as their faces. "If only we had something we could use to cover our noses," sighed Fenway as he lay down on top of some leaves that had fallen off the giant tree.

"Yeah, if only we had some masks," said Patrick as he glanced down at Fenway. Suddenly it hit him. The leaves! If the leaves were big enough to cover their faces, then they would certainly cover their noses.

"Fen, I've got it," Patrick shouted. "The leaves! We can use the leaves as masks. They're big enough."

Fenway shot up and rapidly started wagging his tail. He ran up to Patrick and licked his face excitedly. "Paddy boy! You're a genius," yelled Fenway. "We can even use the rope you brought to tie them snugly to our faces."

They set off to work, quickly making masks out of the leaves on the ground and bits of rope that Patrick had tucked away in his adventure belt. With their masks on, they bravely entered a place where no boy and his dog had gone before: the Stinky Sock Spiral.

Patrick and Fenway made their way through the spiral slowly and carefully. A smelly fog surrounded them—it made it

hard for them to see and breathe. "Blech! This is terrible," said Patrick as he waved his arms around, hoping to clear the air.

"We just have to focus on making it out of here without fainting," said Fenway.

Step by step, bit by bit, the boys walked until they reached a clearing in the spiral. Little did they know, the worst was yet to come. "Finally!" said Patrick, breathing a sigh of relief. "We can breathe and relax." He removed his mask and helped Fenway with his.

The boys looked around a bit. The Stinky Sock Spiral was nothing like the Valley of the Monkeys. This place was quite stinky and very spooky. Patrick and Fenway didn't like it at all. They continued to walk around and breathe in as much clean air as they could, until Patrick came across a tree that was about to bring trouble.

"Hey, Fen, come look at this tree I found," Patrick called. Fenway trotted over to see what Paddy was so excited about.

The tree was something neither had ever seen. Its leaves were a deep shade of emerald green, with white buds that looked like coils. This definitely wasn't like any tree they had back home in Cranston.

"Whoa, this tree is funky. What's that white thing on it?" Fenway asked.

"I don't know. It kinda looks like a flower," Patrick said as he leaned in for a smell.

Suddenly, the white bud began to move and shake. Patrick attempted to run, but it was too late. The bud burst open, spraying him with an awful smell, just like a skunk would do.

Fenway looked on in horror. "It's a stinky sock! Run, Paddy boy! Ruuuun!" Fenway yelled as he pushed Patrick out of the way of the tree.

One by one, the buds began to open. Patrick and Fenway ran as fast as they could, but it was hard to see. As they ran all the way around the spiral, they saw a bay in the distance as the air cleared up.

"Head for the water, Paddy!" Fenway shouted.

They ran as fast as they could toward the bay. They needed to wash up fast or else they would have a hard time explaining their stench to Patrick's mom. But as with every inch of that jungle, a new adventure awaited them in the bay.

SHIVER ME TIMBERS

Patrick and Fenway washed up like they'd never washed up before. They washed behind their ears, and between their fingers, toes, and paws. They scrubbed and scrubbed.

"Can you believe that happened?" Fenway asked excitedly as he stepped out of the water.

"I never want to see or smell another stinky sock ever again for as long as I live!" Patrick shouted.

"That was awful," agreed Fenway as he shook the water off his body.

They managed to wash most of the smell from their bodies. But their adventure was nowhere near over. According to the map, they still had to tackle Lemon Ice Waterfalls before they could reach their treasure. They walked along the bay, plotting their next move and recounting all that had happened to them since they'd arrived. The falls were visible in the distance. They knew they had to get over there fast, before nighttime arrived and they had to return home. Patrick knew he absolutely had to complete his mission. The boys kept walking and talking, without realizing they were being followed. Then suddenly two pirates sprang out of the jungle and startled Patrick and Fenway.

"Aarrrrrrrgh!" yelled the pirates.

"Aaaah!" yelled Patrick and Fenway.

"Argh! Who be ye?" asked the pirate closest to Patrick.

The adventurers were frozen solid. Could this really be happening? Did they just walk into a pirate trap? "M-m-my n-n-name is Patrick, and this is my dog, Fenway," Patrick responded with a look of fear upon his face.

"What business have ye here in the bay?" the other pirate asked.

Patrick and Fenway glanced at each other. They were both too afraid to speak. "Business?" Patrick finally asked.

"Aye!" shouted both pirates.

The boys were frozen in their spots. First tickling monkeys, then stinky socks, and now pirates. Could this adventure get any worse?

"Not willing to speak, eh? Fine. It's off to the captain with ye! He'll make ye speak or walk the plank," said one of the pirates.

The walk to the pirate ship was long. The boys couldn't help but stare at the pirates leading the way. "What do we do now?" Patrick whispered over to Fenway.

"I don't know, Paddy boy," Fenway whispered back, "but I'm sure we'll think of something."

The boys' eyes grew wider and wider as they approached the ship. This ship was *huge*! It had black and gold sails and massive cannons on each side. At the very top was a black flag with gold stripes. Patrick and Fenway gasped at the sight of it. Something told them they were in for a fight.

"All right. Up ye go to see the captain!" said one pirate as he motioned for Patrick and Fenway to walk up the ramp on the side of the ship.

Once aboard, Patrick and Fenway were frozen in place. Hundreds of pirates moved about, getting the ship ready for its next voyage.

"Arrrrgh! Ye two stay put while we fetch the captain," said one of the pirates. With that, the two pirates left the boys among the rest of the crew.

"Now's our chance, Fenway. We can make a run for it," said Patrick.

"Yeah, you're right. Let's get out of here," Fenway replied.

The boys turned and attempted to run as fast as they could. But just before they could make it out, two large hands reached out and lifted them high up into the air. The boys yelled and kicked, but it was no use. Their attempt to escape had failed.

"Ha ha ha ha ha ha ha!" was all the boys could hear from behind them as they struggled to be set free. Then with a loud *crash*, the boys were thrown to the floor of the ship. Laughter roared up all around them. In front of the boys stood a large, plump man with an eye as blue as the sea and a patch on the other. His hair and beard were as yellow as the sun, and his mouth had two gold teeth that shone brightly. He wore a black coat, and has a right leg made of wood. He introduced himself as Captain Pauly Peg Leg.

The captain leaned over, inches away from Patrick and Fenway's faces, and bellowed, "What business have ye on me grand ship, the *Screaming Bull*?"

Fenway tried to answer but couldn't—he was too terrified of the captain. Patrick quivered, but he knew he had to stand up for Fenway and himself. He had to stand up to the captain. He got up, adjusted his hat and belt, and puffed his chest out proudly. *It's now or never*, he thought.

"Captain! My name is Patrick, and this is Fenway. We are two explorers from Rhode Island in search of buried treasure. Today, alone, we were almost tickled to death by monkeys and barely escaped the Stinky Sock Spiral. We've come a long way and just want to find a way to get to our treasure, where gold, diamonds, rubies, and doggie treats await us," said Patrick proudly, nose to nose with the captain.

The captain leaned back and stared at the boys. "So ye be pirates from the Island of Rhode in search of buried treasure,

who fought their way out of that crazy jungle?" asked the captain, wide-eyed.

Patrick glanced over at Fenway, who was standing right beside him as he spoke. "Aye!" Patrick replied proudly.

The captain looked around at his men, who were in awe of Patrick and Fenway's bravery in the jungle. "Well, why didn't ye say so? Welcome aboard, brothers from the Island of Rhode! Any man or beast that can tame the jungle without a sword is welcome on our ship," shouted the captain as the entire crew hollered and cheered.

The captain slapped Patrick and Fenway on the backs to welcome them, and guided them below deck to see how he could help them on their journey. "Do ye have a treasure map to let ye know where ye's going?" the captain asked.

"Yes," said Fenway. "Paddy boy, show him your arm."

Patrick stuck out his cast and revealed the map to the captain. The captain studied the map, tracing the steps of where the boys had been and where they had yet to go. "Can you help us get to our treasure, Captain?" Patrick asked.

The captain stared at their map and rubbed his beard. A look of worry fell upon his face. "Aye. My crew and I are sailing with ye. I know we can be of service to ye. But a word of caution: Lemon Ice Waterfalls isn't as nice as it seems. Something *evil* lurks in its waters. An *evil* I've yet to defeat.

But together we can conquer it. Off we go," said the captain as he made his way above deck to set sail.

THE SLUSHY RIDE HOME

The *Screaming Bull* made its way out of Pirates Bay, toward the buried treasure. But like every other attempt, this voyage was far from over. The farther the ship got from the bay, the colder and rougher the sea became.

"It'ssss f-f-freeeezzzziinng!" said Patrick as his teeth chattered.

"S-s-ssoooo c-c-cooolllddd," said Fenway, shaking.

"Ha ha ha ha! Haven't ye ever felt a cold wind at yer back before?" asked the captain.

Just then, a pirate appeared with a change of clothes for Patrick and Fenway. Now they really looked like pirates. They dressed in long coats with sashes, and Patrick even had an eye patch!

"Ha ha! Now you're both ready to conquer the sea," said the captain.

As the ship sailed on, Patrick and Fenway plotted what their next move would be once they were off the ship. They knew they needed to move fast. They had to get home before sunset, before anyone realized they were gone. Just then, the ship slowed its pace and began to shake. Everyone froze in place. Captain Pauly began to laugh. "Ha ha! It's begun!" he said. Then as quickly as he could, he shouted, "Aye, me mateys, all sailors report to your cannons, grab your swords, and prepare for battle!"

The boys watched as all the pirates scrambled to grab their weapons. "Boys!" yelled the captain. "Here, you'll be needing this." With that, the captain handed Patrick a sword. Whatever was coming their way must be big and strong.

"But why?" Patrick yelled.

The captain pointed, and the boys turned around to see what was shaking the ship. Out of the falls it arose. The thing was *huge*! It had a dome for a head, and out of the dome came many, many arms made of straws; its body was a gigantic red see-through cup. It had mean eyes, and when it growled, blue slush poured out of its mouth.

"What is that, Paddy boy?" Fenway asked as he looked up in horror.

"It's...it's...it's a slushy!" Patrick exclaimed. "A gigantic *slushy*." The monster rose out of the water, screeching and hollering. Blue slushy poured out of its mouth and onto the ship. The pirates were slipping and sliding across the deck.

"Ready, men?" the captain yelled. "Fire the cannons!" he commanded.

The sound of the cannons filled the air. Patrick and Fenway covered their ears and braced themselves alongside the captain. Then all of a sudden, the captain was gone. The monster had picked him up and entangled him in one of his straws.

"Aaaarrrrgh! Ye want to fight?" he yelled at the monster. "Then fight we shall!"

"Oh nooo!" yelled Patrick and Fenway together. The boys stared in shock as the monster held the captain in one of its straws. The captain wiggled and kicked but couldn't free himself from the monster.

"Paddy boy, we have to rescue the captain!" yelled Fenway.

"I know. But how?" Patrick replied. They looked around for a way to help the captain. They noticed one of the slushy's straw arms wrapped around the ship; it led up to where the captain was.

"I've got it!" said Fenway. "I'll try and get the monster's attention. When I do, you run up that straw and go save the captain."

"Do you think it'll work?" Patrick asked.

"We'll never know unless we try, Paddy boy. Are you ready?" asked Fenway.

"It's now or never. Let's do it!" said Patrick as he hooked his sword to his belt.

The boys set about their plan. Fenway ran in circles and jumped all around the slushy-soaked ship, trying to get the monster's attention. "Yoo-hoo! Hey, big guy! Look over here! Look!" yelled Fenway. He kept running and jumping and bouncing off the straws until the monster finally looked. "OK, Paddy boy! Now!" he yelled. With that, Patrick ran forward and up the straw. The monster was still watching Fenway.

"Captain! On the count of three, I'm going to free you!" Patrick yelled.

"Aye, me boy! Do it quickly before the beast sees ye!" the captain replied.

Patrick grabbed his sword and prepared to swing. "One… two…threeee!" Patrick swung the sword with all of his might, slicing right through the straw and freeing the captain. A loud screech filled the air as the monster retreated back into the ocean.

"Paddy boy, you did it!" yelled Fenway as he ran up to Patrick, who'd fallen to the floor along with the captain.

"Ye did it, my boy! You defeated the beast!" yelled the captain.

The crew gathered around Patrick and Fenway and tossed them both in the air in celebration. Just then, one of the sailors yelled, "Land ho!"

The boys jumped for joy. They were moments away from reaching their buried treasure. Once the ship docked, they ran down the ramp with the captain and onto land.

"According to the map, the treasure is straight ahead!" yelled Patrick. He took off running toward the treasure, faster than he ran through Stinky Sock Spiral. Fenway and Captain Pauly tried hard to keep up.

When they got to the spot, they began to dig and dig. Then finally, they heard a loud *thump*. They had found their treasure. Deeper and deeper they dug until it was finally in front of them. It was the biggest treasure chest they'd ever seen! When they opened it, all the gold, gems, jelly beans and doggie treats spilled out. The boys and the captain laughed and cheered at what they'd found. There was enough treasure for them all. Patrick filled his adventure belt with gold coins, jewels, and doggie treats for Fenway. He gave the rest to Captain Pauly and his men. Then the sun began to set, and it was time for the boys to head back.

"Where ye off to now, boys?" the captain asked.

"We have to get back home," said Patrick sadly.

"Aye. Thank ye, boys, for saving me and my ship. I shall never forget it," said Captain Pauly. He gave both Fenway and Patrick a hug and sailed away on the *Screaming Bull*.

"Are you ready to go?" Fenway asked.

"No, but I guess we have to. Here, have a treat for the way home," Patrick replied. "How are we going to get back?"

"Same way we came. We tail it!" said Fenway.

The boys huddled together to begin their journey back home. As Fenway wagged his tail, he said, "We've had our fun. The adventure's done. Let's go back home and plan another one."

The boys opened their eyes and found themselves back in Patrick's room. They looked around and then back at each other. Everything was *exactly* as they'd left it. Suddenly, there was a knock at the door, and Patrick's mom came through. "Hey, pal," she said. "I've been calling out to you for five minutes now. Dinner's ready. Come on!" But before she could turn and walk away, she stopped and said, "What's that smell? I bet your brother left his stinky gym socks out again!"

Patrick turned to Fenway, and they both began to laugh uncontrollably.

THE END

The Adventure Continues...

Congratulations! You've completed your first adventure with Paddy & Fenway. You've followed them from Cranston, to the doctor's office, all the way to the Amazon, and back to Paddy's bedroom! You've conquered the Tickling Monkeys, trenched through the Stinky Sock Spiral, and even made a new friend in Pauly Peg Leg.

But wait! The adventure is not over yet. It seems Paddy has dropped some of his jelly beans along the way! Go back through the illustrations and see if you can help Paddy and Fenway find them all. There is one lost jelly bean in every picture. Remember, they need YOUR help in recovering his tasty beans in order to be ready for their next adventure! Can you help Paddy and Fenway?

About The Author

Patricia Gonzalez is an emerging author who lives in Union City, New Jersey. She has a Bachelor's degree in Media Arts from New Jersey City University in Jersey City, NJ. Her inspiration for the book was drawn from the interactions between her fiancé Patrick and their dog, Fenway.

When she is not busy spending time with Patrick and Fenway, she spends her time reading, writing and taking pictures.

For more information/questions/comments please contact: grandadventuresofpaddyandfen@gmail.com.

Be sure to follow us on social media!
Twitter: @Paddy_Fen
Instagram: @paddyandfenway
Facebook: The Grand Adventures of Paddy and Fenway

About The Illustrator

Ciro W. Romero is a designer and illustrator working out of Hudson County, NJ. Graduating with a Bachelors of Fine Arts Degree in Illustration in 2008, he has since worked in a wide spectrum of fields from animation, graphic design, film, publishing, and illustration.

His work can be seen on Independent Lens, One Kings Lane, Better Home and Gardens Magazine, Advanced Photoshop Magazine, ImagineFX Magazine, UCDA Magazine, and Gothic Magazine.

He enjoys drawing, playing banjo, and drinking espresso with his wife Nicole.

Check out Ciro's work at: www.ciroart.com. Follow him on Facebook at: CiroArt.

Made in the USA
Middletown, DE
06 May 2015